An I Can Read Book®

THE CASE OF THE
Cat's Meow

by Crosby Bonsall

HarperCollins*Publishers*

The Case of the Cat's Meow
Copyright © 1965 by Crosby Bonsall
All rights reserved. No part of this book may be used or reproduced in any
manner whatsoever without written permission except in the case of brief
quotations embodied in critical articles and reviews. Printed in China.
For information address HarperCollins Children's
Books, a division of HarperCollins Publishers, 10 East 53rd Street,
New York, NY 10022.

Library of Congress Catalog Card Number: 65-11451
ISBN 0-06-444017-6 (pbk.)
ISBN 0-06-020561-X (lib. bdg.)
09 10 11 12 13 SCP 10 9

for my mother EMN

 for my sister MNP

and

 for Midnight CAT

Snitch was yelling.

He was pulling a wagon

with a funny thing in it.

And he was yelling.

"Stop yelling,"

yelled his brother, Wizard.

"Stop yelling,"

yelled his friend Skinny.

"Stop yelling,"

yelled his friend Tubby.

8

Snitch stopped yelling.

It was very quiet.

The little noise in the wagon

sounded like a loud cry.

"MEOW!"

9

There, in an old bird cage,

sat Mildred.

Mildred was Snitch's cat.

"I'm keeping her safe," Snitch said.

"Somebody might steal her."

10

"Who wants old Mildred?" Tubby said.

"She's dumb."

"She's no fun," Skinny said.

"She makes too much noise,"

Wizard said.

"She's nice!" Snitch yelled.

"I love Mildred!"

"Nobody is going to steal Mildred,"

Wizard said. "We are private eyes.

We have our own clubhouse.

We have a sign on the door.

Nobody will steal anything.

Take my word for it."

12

"We can catch anybody now,"

Tubby said. "We have an alarm."

"What alarm?" Snitch asked.

"The alarm we just put in,"

Skinny said. "Step over this string."

"See," Wizard said, "if anybody comes sneaking around here, he will trip over this string. That will pull this pail of water down on his head. Then the string on the pail handle will ring this bell."

"And it will ring and ring and ring," Snitch cried. "And we will catch whoever wants to steal Mildred."

"Nobody wants to steal Mildred," Wizard said. "Take my word for it."

Snitch started to yell.

"Come on," said Wizard.

"It's almost time for supper."

"I knew it must be," Tubby said.

They stepped over the string.

Nobody wanted to set off the alarm.

When Snitch and Wizard got home,

Mildred ran up the back steps.

She ran in the little door

in the big door

that was her door.

"She's nice," Snitch said.

"I love Mildred."

17

But did Mildred love Snitch?

The next morning she didn't come

when Snitch called her.

He called and called and called.

18

Wizard looked out the window.

"Somebody stole Mildred,"

Snitch yelled.

"Nobody stole Mildred," Wizard said.

"Take my word for it."

But he came down in a hurry.

"I'll call Skinny and Tubby,"

Wizard said.

"They will help us find Mildred."

"Somebody stole her," Snitch said.

And he started to yell.

The boys looked for Mildred

all that day.

"Anybody seen a dumb cat?"

Tubby asked.

"Anybody seen a cat?"

Skinny asked.

"She doesn't do much."

"Anybody seen a noisy cat?"
Wizard asked.

23

"Have you seen my cat Mildred?"

Snitch asked.

"She's soft and she's nice.

And I love her."

But he did not find Mildred.

Nobody found Mildred.

Nobody had even seen Mildred.

24

Back at the clubhouse Wizard said,
"We are not very good private eyes
if we can't find Mildred."
"But how can we?" Skinny asked.
"Food!" Tubby said.
"Mildred has to eat."

25

"That's a good idea," said Wizard.

"Tonight we'll put food in the yard.

If Mildred is hungry, she'll come home."

"She likes liver," Snitch said,

"and strawberry jelly. Without seeds."

"*I* like strawberry jelly," Tubby said.

Each of the boys

brought some food.

Next day they had cats, all right.

They had cats in the tree,

cats on the roof.

They had cats on the grass

and one cat

sitting on a stone

in the middle of the brook.

But no Mildred.

"Our plan was no good," Wizard said.

"How do we get rid of these cats?"

"I know!" Skinny cried. "Dogs!

Dogs will chase the cats away."

"They will scare Mildred,"

Snitch said.

"Mildred isn't here," Wizard said.

Snitch started to yell again.

30

The boys brought every dog

they could find on the block.

They got rid of the cats, all right.

But now they had dogs.

They had dogs in the tree,

dogs on the roof.

They had dogs on the grass

and one dog

sitting on a stone

in the middle of the brook.

And it took the rest of the day

to take the dogs home.

After supper Wizard called a meeting.
"We have to keep our eyes open
day and night," he said.
"Let's ask if we can sleep
in the yard tonight."

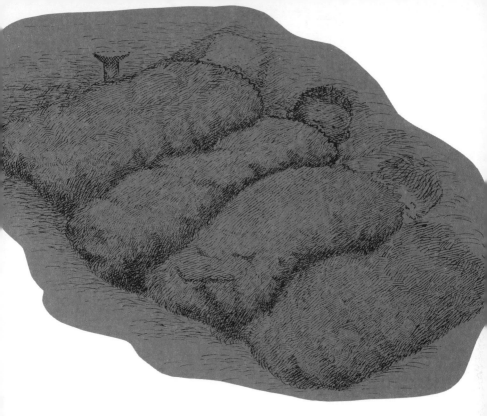

They went to bed

even before their bedtime.

They liked being outdoors.

It was warm.

The sky was full of stars.

Soon each of them was sound asleep.

And that was when the alarm went off.

The bell rang and rang.

Wizard was up first.

And then Skinny.

Tubby got stuck in his sleeping bag.

So he took it with him.

Wizard turned on his flashlight.

There was Snitch.

"I heard someone stealing Mildred," he said.

"You can't steal a cat who is not here!" Wizard yelled.

But they all went into the house for the rest of the night.

Next day Snitch told them something.

"Last night I put food

in Mildred's dish.

And now it's gone!"

Wizard was mad

because he had not thought

of Mildred's dish.

41

But he had a plan.

That night he put Mildred's dish

on a cookie tin filled with flour.

"Whoever is eating the food

will have to walk over the flour."

"And the white feet will leave

a trail we can follow," Skinny cried.

Next morning the food was gone.

But there were clear white paw prints

going down the steps.

43

Then the paw prints stopped.

"Shucks," Tubby cried,

"the flour didn't last long enough."

And Snitch started to yell.

"What will we do now?" Skinny asked.

"Try again tonight," Wizard said.

"And we will lock Mildred's door."

"Why?" asked Tubby.

"That cat is so noisy," Wizard said,

"she will cry if she can't get in."

"And we'll hear her," Tubby said.

"And the case will be solved."

"Then we'll be private ears,"

Skinny said.

That night the boys met on the porch.

"Now let's keep our eyes open,"

Wizard said.

They went to bed early.

But the night was warm

and the sky was full of stars.

Soon they were sound asleep.

"What was that?" Tubby whispered.

"Just an old cat," Snitch said.

He started to go back to sleep.

"A CAT!" he shouted.

"It's Mildred! She is found!"

Wizard turned on his flashlight.

It was Mildred, all right.

But she was going away.

"Meow," she said as she left.

51

"Follow that cat," Wizard yelled.

Down the steps they ran,

over the grass, up to the clubhouse.

Mildred was one jump ahead of them.

One more jump took her

over the string.

The string that was part

of the alarm.

"Some alarm!" Wizard said.

"It sure doesn't catch cats!"

Each boy stepped over the string.

Mildred jumped into the basket

in the corner.

"Where's Mildred?" cried Snitch.

"I brought her supper."

"The case is solved," said Wizard.

"I told you nobody stole her."

Snitch ran over to the basket.

He started to yell again.

"MILDRED HAS KITTENS!"

58

"Oh, boy, I want one," Tubby cried.

"Me too," said Skinny.

"Don't forget me," Wizard said.

But Snitch had his arms

around the basket.

"Tubby said Mildred was dumb,"
Snitch said.

"Skinny said she was no fun.

Wizard said she made too much noise."

Well, they *had* said all those things.

Right then they changed their minds.

Mildred was nice. They loved her.

And so they waited for the kittens

to grow old enough

to leave their mother.

When they were old enough

Snitch gave a kitten

to each private eye.

"This is one case

I'm glad we solved," Skinny said.

"It's lucky," said Tubby,

"we're such good private eyes.

The alarm didn't help us."

"Snitch was the only one

we ever caught with it," Wizard said.

"Mildred will take care of us now,"

Snitch said.

"No, *my* cat will," said Tubby.

"No, *my* cat will," said Skinny.

"No, *my* cat will," said Wizard.

"You can take my word for it."

And Snitch was yelling again.